IT WAS A DARK AND STORMY NIGHT

Alphonse

Giorgio

It was a Dark

Janet and Allan Ahlberg

Fabrizzi

and Stormy Night

PUFFIN BOOKS

Leonardo   *Luigi*

PUFFIN BOOKS

Published by the Penguin Group
Penguin Books Ltd, 27 Wrights Lane, London W8 5TZ, England
Penguin Putnam Inc., 375 Hudson Street, New York, New York 10014, USA
Penguin Books Australia Ltd, Ringwood, Victoria, Australia
Penguin Books Canada Ltd, 10 Alcorn Avenue, Toronto, Ontario, Canada M4V 3B2
Penguin Books (NZ) Ltd, Private Bag 102902, NSMC, Auckland, New Zealand

Penguin Books Ltd, Registered Offices: Harmondsworth, Middlesex, England

First published by Viking 1993
Published in Picture Puffin 1994
Published in this edition 1998
9 10 8

Text and illustrations copyright © Janet and Allan Ahlberg, 1993
All rights reserved

Consultant Designer: Douglas Martin

The moral right of the author and illustrator has been asserted

Typeset in Poliphilus

Printed in Singapore by Imago

British Library Cataloguing in Publication Data
A CIP catalogue record for this book is available from the British Library

ISBN 0–141–30027–2

Contents

Higgins

The Mighty Chief

For Douglas Martin

CHAPTER ONE

Antonio and the Brigands

IT WAS A dark and stormy night, the
rain came down in torrents, there were
brigands on the mountains, and
wolves, and the chief of the brigands said
to Antonio, 'I'm bored – tell us a story!'

Antonio was a small brave boy, eight years old, who had been kidnapped by the brigands and carried off to their secret cave. He scratched his curly head, puffed out his cheeks and said, 'I don't know any stories.'

'Make one up,' growled the chief.

'Yeah,' said the brigands. 'Begin at the beginning.'

'Right-o!' Antonio said, and he paused for a moment – and began his story.

'It was a dark and stormy night,' said Antonio. (It was all he could think of.) 'The rain came down in torrents. There were brigands on the mountains, and wolves, and the chief of the brigands said –'

At this point, the real chief held up his hands. 'Get rid of the rain.'

'I beg your pardon?' Antonio looked puzzled.

'No rain,' said the chief. 'I'm sick of it.'

'Yeah,' said the brigands. 'Let's have a dry story.'

Once more Antonio paused; and then, 'Right-o! How about this: It was a cold and frosty night, the snow swirled down around the entrance to the cave, and there were wolves on the mountains, and bears –'

'Bears as well?' said the brigands.

'And the wolves and bears crept ever closer to the entrance to the cave, where only a hissing, crackling fire kept them at bay.'

Meanwhile, outside, the real rain rattled down and the real wolves shook their sodden fur.

'Hang on a minute.' The chief tossed a log onto the fire.

'And the chief tossed a log onto the fire,' said Antonio.

The chief blew his nose.

'And blew his nose –'

'Stop that!' said the chief.

'And all the while the pile of logs got smaller and smaller,' Antonio continued, 'and the fire burnt lower and lower, and

the wolves and bears crept nearer and nearer and nearer . . .'

'Ooh!' cried the brigands.

'Finally the fire went – out! And the wolves and bears came rushing in, opened wide their hungry jaws and –'

'I'm fed up with wolves,' said the chief.

'Bears, too,' said the brigands.

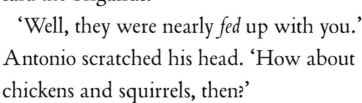

'Well, they were nearly *fed* up with you.' Antonio scratched his head. 'How about chickens and squirrels, then?'

'Don't be cheeky.' The chief mopped his brow with the same spotty hanky with which he had previously blown his nose.

'Anyway, I'm also fed up with caves.'

'And mountains,' added the brigands. 'Let's have a flatter story.'

By the way, in case you were wondering, Antonio had been captured by the brigands — all six of them — that very evening down in the valley. He was supposed to have been guarding his family's goats, but had been caught napping and *kid*napped by the brigands. They kidnapped a couple of kids, too (baby goats, that is), *and* stole a line of washing. Now, with lanterns flickering in the high wind and rain lashing their faces, Antonio's deeply worried parents, Mr and Mrs Panetta, were out upon the mountainside searching for him.

CHAPTER TWO

The Preposterous Ambush

ANTONIO PUFFED OUT his cheeks and fidgeted. Firelight flickered on the glittering daggers and polished pistol butts of the brigands, which, I may say, were just about the only things

they ever cleaned. Their hands were
dirty, the backs of their necks dirtier
still, and nowhere in that cave was there
a toothbrush to be seen.

For the third time, Antonio began his
story. 'Right-o! It was a bright and
starry night.'

'That's better,' said the chief.

'The silver moon shone down upon the
silver beach beside the silver sea.'

17

'Ah!' sighed the brigands, and one of them – Giorgio – added, 'I love silver.'

'Suddenly, lumbering towards the mighty chief and his brigand band as they sat quietly dozing on the silver sand –'

'That rhymes!' observed the chief, admiringly.

'– came half a dozen hungry bears.'

At once the brigands protested. 'Not bears again!'

'We said no bears!'

'Bears – on a beach? That's silly.'

'All right, then – pirates,' said Antonio. 'Cut-throat pirates charging up across the sand from the left, and South American ruffians –'

'What kind of beach is this?' said the chief.

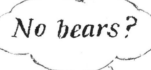

'– racing in from the right – and massive sharks churning up the waters of the bay,

and . . .' Antonio cudgelled his brain for more ideas. 'A crocodile-infested swamp behind them, killer parrots in the palm trees, and . . . and . . .' He paused again to catch his breath and work out, if he could, what happened next.

'What happened next?' said the chief.

'Well, the chief and his brigands put up a brave fight –'

'Of course they did,' said the chief.

'– but it was no use.'

'What do you mean, "no use"?'

'They were surrounded and outnumbered.'

'So what?' said the chief.

'Cut up with cutlasses, porcupined with arrows –'

'That's a good word,' said Fabrizzi, another brigand.

'– swallowed alive by sharks and crocodiles, pecked by –'

'Pecked nothing!' The disgruntled chief staggered to his feet. 'I'll tell you what *really* happened.'

'Yeah – tell him, Chief!' cried the brigands.

'The chief said,' said the chief, taking
over the story, '"Come on, men —
follow me!" Whereupon, without
flinching and with never a thought
for his own safety, the mighty chief

battled his way through that
preposterous ambush. With one arm
tied behind me – I mean, him – he
wiped the beach with the pirate chief,
the ruffian chief, and the shark and

crocodile chiefs, come to that.'

'And the parrot chief, Chief?' said the brigands.

'And him. After that, he led his grateful band of brigands —'

'Three cheers for the chief!' yelled Giorgio.

'— his grateful band to . . .' At this point the chief's hitherto lively invention began to falter. '. . . to, er, a place of safety.'

'What place, Chief?' inquired the brigands.

'Er . . . a castle.'

'What — on a beach?' said Antonio.

'Why not?' said the chief. 'It's better than bears.'

'Perhaps it was a sand-castle!' cried Fabrizzi, thinking to join in the fun. But the mighty chief was not amused. He banged Fabrizzi on the head with a wooden spoon, a rather greasy wooden spoon as it happens, lately used for stirring a rather greasy stew.

After that, with the spoon conveniently in his hand, the chief took the opportunity to give the stew a further stir. The big black pot, encrusted with previous generations of stew, was bubbling sluggishly ('Like a hot swamp,' thought Antonio) as it hung suspended from a hook above the fire.

Antonio watched the chief and the chief's enormous wavering shadow on the wall of the cave.

He glanced around at the shadowy piles
of stolen goods stacked everywhere: a
broken bicycle, dozens of pairs (or half-
pairs) of boots, an orange tree in a brass
pot, a brass bed, an enormous tin-plated
megaphone, a barrel of wine, a
considerable number of clockwork
toys (which Alphonse – one of the
brigands – had a passion for), a trio of
trussed-up chickens, and Antonio's own
little goats tethered towards the rear of
the cave. As far as Antonio could see in
the gloom (and the smoke), they were
nibbling a straw hat. Oh, and there

was the stolen washing, still on its line
and hanging up to dry across the cave.

Meanwhile, down in the valley Mr and
Mrs Panetta were drying out as well, and
drinking coffee in the kitchen, and
wondering what to do. Antonio's four little
sisters were peeping at them from the stairs.
The rain had eased and dawn itself was not
far off. And the wolves – the real wolves –
had slunk away.

CHAPTER THREE

The Thingy

ACK IN THE cave, the chief
raised the spoon to his lips, pulled
a face (the brigands were nifty
thieves but hopeless cooks) and turned
to Antonio. 'Keep on with the story.
They're in the castle.'

Antonio took up his cue. 'Right-o! They're in the castle.'

'But no more cutlasses, mind. No crocodiles or sharks – no jaws!'

'No bears' jaws either,' said the brigands.

'No . . . violence,' Fabrizzi said.

'Right-o!' Antonio clasped his hands together. 'So then the chief and his merry men' ('That's Robin Hood!' exclaimed Alphonse) 'escaped from the pursuing pirates et cetera, crocodiles and ruffians et cetera, et cetera, pulled up the drawbridge of their high and handsome castle, and got clean away.'

'What about the parrots, though?' said Luigi, another of the brigands. 'They could fly over and –'

'Forget the parrots,' said the chief.

'Well, there they were in the castle, which, as I have said, was high, wide and handsome.'

'He never said "wide",' said Fabrizzi.

'Unfortunately, however, it was also clammy, cold . . . and creepy.'

'Ooh!' cried the brigands.

'Yes – creepy. There were mysterious clankings in the dungeons, headless people on the battlements, pictures with moving eyes in the great hall, ghosts in armour, and – worst of all – a . . . a . . . a *Thingy* in the moat.'

'A Thingy?' said the brigands. 'What's a . . . Thingy?'

'Nobody knows,' Antonio let his

31

voice get deep and echoey, 'or ever lived to tell.'

'Hang on,' said the chief. 'If nobody knows, logically speaking, how can you say it was there?'

'Because it *was*,' intoned Antonio.

'He's contradicted himself there,' said Alphonse.

'Because the brigands and their mighty chief *saw* it, and ever after wished they hadn't.'

'Did they?' said the brigands.

'Yes. Because at midnight, as the black bats squeaked and flittered overhead, the awful Thingy left its watery lair and came out dripping up the stair' ('Rhyming again!' said the chief) '. . . to get them.'

'Ooh!' cried the brigands; and then,
'It's not true, though, is it?'

'Anyway, the drawbridge was up,' said
Alphonse.

'It smashed it down,' Antonio said.

'They escaped into the keep.'

'Smashed that down as well.'

'Shot it, then!'

'Bulletproof skin.'

'With a cannon!'

'Missed.'

35

At this point, the exasperated chief
banged his wooden spoon against the
side of the stewpot and snapped the end
off. 'All right, they strangled it with its
own braces – who cares?' He gestured
wildly with the stump of the spoon and
looked accusingly at the brigands. 'What I
want to know is, whose bright idea was it
to kidnap this little pest in the first place?'

'Giorgio's!' said Luigi.

'Fabrizzi's!' said Giorgio.

'Higgins's!' said Fabrizzi.

(Of course, the truth is it was the chief's idea.)

Higgins, by the way, as you will doubtless have guessed, was an English brigand. How he came to be half-way up a mountain in southern Italy, complete with mustachios, bandoleers and golden earrings, is an even better story than this one, in my opinion. He started out as a schoolmaster, for instance, I can tell you that. However, space is limited, time is pressing, the chief's still in the middle of his rage (though it's moving now towards a sulk), and so . . .

'I'll tell you this,' said the chief. 'I'm writing no ransom notes for him.'

'Oh, go on, Chief,' said Leonardo, the last of the brigands.

'No – waste of time. Boy like this – they'd pay money to lose him.' Actually, the chief was relieved not to be writing a note. He found writing a strain. No matter how many pens he stole, they all blotted, and spelling made his head ache.

The chief sat down with a sulky expression on his face. 'I mean, you ask him for a simple story, and what do you get? Rubbish.'

'And bears all the time,' said Giorgio.

'And . . . violence,' Fabrizzi said.

'Ah, but the Thingy has no teeth, y'know,' Antonio explained. 'It sort of sucks people to –'

'I don't want to hear it.' The chief turned his face to the wall and hunched his shoulders in an even deeper sulk.

For a time a heavy silence hung in the cave. The fire crackled, the little goats crunched up the last of the straw hat, Fabrizzi burped, and Giorgio smothered a laugh.

CHAPTER FOUR

Feasts and Treasure

OUTSIDE A LIGHT wind was blowing the last of the storm clouds away. In the east there was a glow, and streaks of pink and violet and duck-egg green tinged the darker edge of

the sky. Elsewhere on the mountain the
real wolves were curling up, snug and
almost dry now in *their* cave, preparing
to sleep out the day. This is the way of
things with predators, wolves and
brigands both, night-workers the lot of
them; except, in the brigands' case,
when it rained. And if you are thinking,
it was late for Antonio to be up – or
nearly time to be *getting* up – well, so it

was. Not that he minded; being up late, I mean. At home it was the goal of his life.

Back in the cave, the brigands were exchanging anxious looks. (Somehow, when the chief was suffering, he had a way of passing it on to them.) Each gestured to the others to *do* something.

Finally, up spoke Giorgio. 'Let's give him one more chance, Chief.'

'Yeah,' said Fabrizzi. 'One more story – something nice – something pleasant.

What d'y'say?'

The chief responded with a huffy
movement of his shoulders.

The brigands gestured to Antonio to
make a start. 'He's got just the thing,
Chief,' said Alphonse. 'Listen to this!'

'Yes,' said Antonio, 'er . . . just the
thing . . . er . . . er . . . a banquet!'

'A banquet!' shouted the brigands, determined to be delighted.

'I can't wait!' cried Giorgio.

'Yes, the biggest banquet anybody ever saw.'

'What was there to eat, then?' said the brigands.

'What *wasn't* there to eat,' said Antonio. 'Why, there was –'

Now, at last, the chief spoke. 'Yes, but what about the Thingy?'

'No problem,' said Antonio (while in that selfsame instant thinking, 'I'm getting better at this story-telling all the time'). 'No problem, the chief – the mighty chief – just grabbed the Thingy and, with one hand tied behind him, knocked it cold with the other, strangled

it with its own braces, and tossed it
back into the moat.'

'Bravo!' shouted the brigands.

The chief turned slightly, scowling
still. 'Then what?'

'Then what? Then – the celebration!
A great feast in the banqueting hall:
roast suckling pig and pheasant pie,
mixed meat kebabs, cuttlefish
cutlets –'

'No Brussels sprouts!' said Fabrizzi.

'None,' Antonio said. 'Nor cabbage.'

'Roast potatoes, though,' said
Alphonse.

'Yes, tons of them, all crisp and golden
– and piping-hot, freshly made spaghetti,
tagliatelle, vermicelli, macaroni – and,
best of all, perhaps, a huge tureen of

delicious and enticing stew.'
(Meanwhile, the real stew
plopped and wallowed
in its pot above
the fire, enticing no
one.) 'And after that: marinated
pomegranates – Florentine wafers in soft
meringue – chocolate carnival cake –
Marsala tart with strawberries – treacle
sponge –'

'Oh, treacle
sponge,' said
Giorgio. 'I love it.'

'And doughnuts,'
said Antonio,
'and ice-cream,
and –'

'What flavours?' The chief had turned round completely now, and more or less lost his scowl, i.e. just looked normally menacing.

'Let's have chocolate mint –' began Fabrizzi, but the others shushed him.

'What flavours would you like?' said Antonio.

'Neapolitan,' said the chief.

'Neapolitan?' Antonio puffed out his

cheeks. 'Amazing – that's mostly what
it was, bowls and bowls of it.' He caught
the rueful expression on Fabrizzi's face.
'Well, with a little chocolate mint chip
too, perhaps.'

Fabrizzi beamed.

'And then – the cheese!' Antonio
declared. 'Camembert and Brie – and
Gorgonzola. And wine – Chianti by the
gallon, poured into crystal goblets.'

'Lovely!' cried Luigi. 'I could do with
a drink.'

'And after *that*,' Antonio said, 'the
games!'

'Games?' said Giorgio. 'I'm too full
to move.'

'Me too,' Fabrizzi said. 'I'll burst.'

'No, let's play,' said the chief, now fully

recovered, it seemed, and back in charge.
And he said, 'What games?'

'Pass the Parcel,' said Antonio.

'No,' said the chief.

'Simon Says.'

'No.'

'Blindman's Buff – Musical Chairs –
Treasure Hunt – Spin the –'

'That's the
one,' said the
chief. 'Treasure
Hunt.'

'Yeah, *treasure*.' Alphonse rolled the word around in his mouth and rubbed his hands.

'Right-o!' Antonio said. 'When the

feast was ended, the mighty chief and his
bulging brigands' ('Ha!' cried the
brigands) 'left the washing-up and spread
out through the castle to hunt for treasure.'

'Did they have clues?' said Luigi. 'Lots – maps and all sorts. And the treasure' ('Was it

real?' said Alphonse) 'that they presently found was utterly amazing: massive chests of gold and silver' ('I love it,' said Giorgio) 'and jewels in abundance – by the sackful! – rubies, emeralds, amethysts,

pearls — and diamonds of enormous
size.'

'Bags I the pearls,' said Fabrizzi.

'Bags I the rubies,' Leonardo said.

'Well, they brought the treasure back
into the banqueting hall — yes, staggered

in with it, spread it out upon the floor, where it glittered and shone – and shared it out.'

'No, they didn't,' said the chief.

'One for you and one for me.'

'No,' said the chief. 'You got that wrong. It's the first law of brigandry: any treasure is the chief's.'

'What about finders keepers?'

'That's it,' said the chief. 'They find it; I keep it.'

CHAPTER FIVE

Gorgonzola

ONCE MORE SILENCE returned to the cave. The brigands shuffled uncomfortably in their places and sought to avoid the chief's gaze.

'So . . . er, well,' said Antonio, 'they were going to share it out, only then the

mighty chief said, no, it was *all* his, and
he gathered it up, every last ruby and
pearl, into a huge sack, and tied it up
with a rope – and sat on it.'

'Don't seem fair,' muttered Fabrizzi.

'What was that?' said the chief.

Fabrizzi ducked his head and pretended to search for something in his pockets.

Antonio, seeing a chance to stir things up a little, continued his story. 'Then straight away Fabrizzi leapt onto the banqueting table, kicking the dirty plates

aside, and he said, "It doesn't seem fair!"'

'No, he never!' cried Fabrizzi.

'Yes, he did – and he said, "Why
should the chief get all the treasure?"'

'Oh, shut up, Fabrizzi,' groaned
Fabrizzi.

'After that, Giorgio leapt onto the table'
('No!' protested Giorgio) 'and he said,
"I agree with Fabrizzi! And what I say is,
if the law says that the chief gets all
the treasure, let's take it in turns to be the
chief." "Bravo!" cried Luigi and
Leonardo and Alphonse and Higgins,
and *they* leapt onto the table.'

At that moment, Higgins – the real
Higgins – made his first and, as it turned
out, only contribution to the proceedings.
'I know, let's have a vote.'

'Vote?' growled the chief. '*Vote?* Take it in turns? What's all this? I've been the chief for years, and my father before me. Your father was a baker, Giorgio – and yours, a band-leader – and *yours*, Fabrizzi, a carabiniere!' (i.e. a policeman.)

Fabrizzi hung his head in shame, while Giorgio, to console him, whispered, 'Yes, but his mother was a brigand.'

'Anyway,' Antonio was determined to complete his story, '*then* what happened was, the mighty chief rose to his feet and he said, "Silence, scum!" But the brigands weren't having this. "Don't you call us scum, you old trout!" cried Fabrizzi.'

And the real chief to the real Fabrizzi said, 'Fabrizzi!'

'And Fabrizzi,' said Antonio, 'Fabrizzi, driven beyond endurance, picked up a lump of Gorgonzola from the cheeseboard and hurled it at the chief.'

'And missed,' said the chief.

'And hit him in the eye!'

Whereupon, Giorgio – the real Giorgio – to his own obvious dismay, failed to smother his laughter this time, and burst out with it.

And that did it, probably. More than the insults or the Thingy, more than the Gorgonzola even, *being laughed at* pushed the mighty chief over the precipice of his own temper and into a tremendous rage. His face went red, then purple, and his beard bristled. 'No respect!' he spluttered. He lurched across the cave. 'I'll get you,

Giorgio! And you, Fabrizzi! And you –
and you!'

However, in his haste to be revenged,
the chief dislodged the stewpot from its
hook. At which point, the stew poured
out upon the fire, and a stewy fog
immediately enveloped the cave. The fire
went out and, rapidly, in search of safer
places, so did the brigands, though not
before they had collided many times
('Ow!' yelled Giorgio), and trodden on

each other's toes ('That really hurt!' bawled Alphonse), and terrified themselves ('What's *that*?' Fabrizzi cried) with items of stolen washing dangling from the line.

Meanwhile, the chief – the mighty chief – uttering unprintable threats, had also blundered about in the confusion. He got pecked a couple of times by the trussed-up chickens, which had struggled free. He skidded in the mess of stew upon the floor, trod on and flattened any number of clockwork toys, and – eventually – followed his fellow brigands out. Then, by and by, as the clouds of not-too-fragrant fog dispersed, Antonio – unnoticed and forgotten – made his way out. *On* the way, he tripped over, and subsequently picked up, the enormous tin-plated megaphone.

As Antonio stood at the entrance to the cave in the early morning light looking down into the valley, an interesting scene presented itself. A line of leaping, scrambling brigands was tumbling down the hillside with a wildly gesturing and loudly swearing mighty chief in hot pursuit. Antonio studied the scene for a moment and slowly raised the megaphone to his mouth.

CHAPTER SIX

Antonio and the Megaphone

DOWN THE SLOPE

THE BRIGANDS AND the chief
ran down the slope ('THE
BRIGANDS AND THE CHIEF
RAN DOWN THE SLOPE!' announced
Antonio), blundering into thorns and

stinging nettles ('BLUNDERING INTO THORNS AND STINGING NETTLES!') and grazing their shins and knees on the sharp rocks ('AND GRAZING THEIR SHINS AND KNEES ON THE SHARP ROCKS!'). They came to the river ('CAME TO THE RIVER!'), plunged in ('PLUNGED IN!') and struggled through its icy waters to the further bank ('ITS ICY WATERS TO THE FURTHER BANK!'). Then on they ran ('THEY RAN!') and ran and ran ('AND RAN!'). And from that day to this, or so the story goes, they never came back ('THEY NEVER CAME BACK!').

Antonio's megaphoned voice

('That's a good word,' he thought)
boomed out across the valley. The tiny
distant dripping figure of the puffed-out
chief turned and shook his fist. 'You can
say that again!' he yelled.

'AND NEVER CAME BACK!'
Antonio replied. After that he
untethered the little goats, tucked an
abandoned dagger into his belt for a
souvenir and descended the steep path
to his parents' farmhouse.

In the bright, white kitchen Mr and
Mrs Panetta were preparing to renew
their search. Antonio's sisters, still in
their nighties, were gathered at the
breakfast table dipping crisp golden
rolls into dishes of hot chocolate.

Antonio could smell the chocolate
even before he opened the door, and the
rolls, too. Well, no sooner had he
appeared than his mamma and pappa
grabbed him, and hugged and kissed

him for coming back, and shook and
scolded him for going away.

'But I was kidnapped, Mamma!'
protested Antonio, as his sisters formed
a warm and chocolatey scrum around
him.

'A likely tale,' his pappa said.

'By brigands!' Antonio cried, and he laid his brigand's dagger on the table as proof.

Later, Antonio sat at the table with his own rolls and chocolate, to be followed shortly after by a boiled egg, a toasted Mozzarella sandwich, a couple of peaches (freshly picked), and more chocolate. ('Better than a banquet!' he thought.) His sisters sat beside him, their chins cupped in their hands, their huge eyes fixed on his face.

'Tell us about the brigands!' they cried.

'And the mighty chief!'

'And the cave!'

'Yes – tell us a story.'

Antonio paused and licked a dribble of chocolate from his chin. The kitchen was quiet. His mamma and pappa were watching him, too. 'Right-o!' Antonio said, and he pushed his cup and plate aside, licked his lips just one more time – and began his story.

'It was a dark and stormy night . . .'

This brilliant book is brought to you by two other people who have told stories almost as well as Antonio. One of Britain's most talented author/illustrator teams, Janet and Allan Ahlberg have produced an impressive array of award-winning books, including *Each Peach Pear Plum*, *Peepo!* and *The Jolly Postman*. Allan lives with his daughter, Jessica, near Leicester. Janet died in November 1994.